Oscar and Mercy were becoming well-adjusted to ferry life. It was so wonderfully simple; they ate, they slept and they enjoyed spending time with all their old friends.

One day they were playing on deck when they smelt a delicious mouse. They started following the strong scent, which led them off the ferry and onto land they didn't recognise at all.

They looked around and could see lots of old thatched houses. They sniffed and could smell peaty smoke.

"This must be a Hebridean island," said Oscar, his whiskers twitching with anticipation.

They continued chasing the mouse over heathery hills and peaty earth, but just as they were getting close, it scurried into a hole and disappeared. They looked around, but could see nothing except a running river nearby.

"What do we do now?" cried Mercy, panicking.

"Let's follow this river," Oscar suggested. "It should lead us to the sea and, hopefully, our ferry."

So they followed the river's winding path until, finally, they heard crashing waves. Sure enough, they had reached a beach and the sea.

It wasn't any ordinary beach though. It was littered with lots of people, all bent over and clutching long, thin objects.

"What are they doing?" Oscar asked.

"I don't know, but they look like they're searching for something in the sand," Mercy replied.

"Excuse me," said Oscar, plucking up courage to speak to a man nearby. "What are those people doing?"

"Looking for cockles," the man replied. "They rake the sand until they see a cockle in their prongs, and pick it up as quickly as possible before it gets away."

"Let's go and look," Oscar said. Mercy purred in agreement. The cats hopped down the rocks to the sand. As master hunters, they thought they could show the humans a thing or two about how to catch cockles. Suddenly, though, they noticed the most beautiful-looking cove in the corner of the beach, right where the river met the sea. It looked deserted.

As they looked closer, they spotted a girl all on her own, busily raking away.

"She'd better be careful or she will get cut off as the tide comes in," Mercy remarked sensibly.

Her beautiful voice was being carried across the wind towards them, *"...singing cockles and mussels, alive, alive oh..."*

"She has the voice of an angel," whispered Mercy. They stood transfixed and watched for some time, while the girl carried on, seemingly oblivious to the danger she was in.

“We must warn her!” said Mercy anxiously.

“How can we do that?” Oscar asked.

“We miaow,” Mercy suggested.

The two cats tried miaowing loudly, but the girl couldn’t hear them.

“We must get nearer,” Mercy said. They started walking through the rising tide but, as you probably know, cats don’t like getting wet very much, so they quickly stopped. “What do we do now?” Oscar asked.

“Just think happy thoughts. Then miaow and swim!” Mercy replied.

So, dreaming of mice, they miaowed and swam, and swam and miaowed until finally they reached the cove. As they raced over to the girl, they shouted, "The tide is coming in and you are nearly cut off! Come with us and we will help you." The girl looked around and, suddenly aware of her surroundings, let out a little gasp of fear.

She followed the cats as they raced towards the rising water and started swimming back. They looked such a funny sight – a girl grasping two cats like floats as they swam along!

The current was very strong and Mercy, who was the weakest swimmer of the group, gradually felt herself being pulled away from the others towards the open ocean. "Help!" she screamed.

The girl, having reached the safety of the rocks, clambered over them until she was in line with Mercy. She stretched out her rake as far it would go. “Grab hold!” she shouted. Mercy dug her claws into the rake and held on for dear life as she was pulled out of the gushing water to safety.

Mercy leapt into the girl's arms and curled up into a wet, shaking ball.

"You saved my life," the girl said gently. "How can I ever thank you! I'm Morag, but now is not the time for introductions. Oh, look at you both." The cats shook their soaking wet bodies. "Let's get home and dry you off." She hurriedly led her sodden, dripping troupe towards her cottage nearby.

Much later, they were sipping hot chocolate in front of a roaring fire."I have a present for you both to say thank you," Morag announced. "A cowrie necklace for you," which she presented to Mercy, "and a seaweed bow tie for you," which she carefully tied around Oscar's neck. "Now, sleep well and tomorrow you will go home."

The next day there was such a hullabaloo on the ferry to welcome them back! Everyone wanted to hear about Oscar and Mercy's adventures. They had to tell their story at least twenty times until the captain said, "Skinny malinky long claws, big furry feet... what adventures you two have had... you deserve a treat."

And what a party they had, all night long.

Also available Oscar the Ferry Cat

These stories really grow on you, so they are a delight to read again and again. The pictures brilliantly inform the words and the words create the momentum so the book becomes both a page turner and something to linger over.

Nicholas Ross

What a treat to have Oscar back!
Alexander McCall Smith

A hymn to wild places and furry friends.
Abi Elphinstone, author of *Sky Song*